P9-BYV-740

THE Very Best Doll

JULIA NOONAN

DUTTON CHILDREN'S BOOKS
NEW YORK

With love to Marie and her doll, Mary Jane

My special thanks to Luciana Skinner for her help.

CIP Data is available.

Published in the United States by Dutton Children's Books,
a division of Penguin Young Readers Group
345 Hudson Street, New York, New York 10014
www.penguin.com

Designed by Gloria Cheng

Manufactured in China
First Edition
1 3 5 7 9 10 8 6 4 2
ISBN 0-525-47075-1

Nell was a just-right kind of doll.

A show-lots-of-wear,

always-been-there,

soft-cloth kind of doll.

A play-in-the-flowers,

talk-to-for-hours,

dream-with kind of doll.

A sunshine-or-rain,
never-complain,
loyal kind of doll.

A kiss-on-the-head,

snuggle-in-bed,

smell-right kind of doll.

Then came a new doll.
A big-gift-for-you doll,
silk-dress-of-blue doll,
birthday surprise.

An I-am-the-best doll,
tea-party-guest doll,

every-girl-wants-one,
beautiful doll.

A stylable-hair doll,
rather-not-share doll,
has-her-own-wardrobe,
dressy new doll.

Oh! What a playtime!
Best-doll-all-day time.

Oh! What a birthday...

...till it was night.

Someone is yearning,
tossing and turning.

Something is missing.

Someone feels sad.

"I need my old doll,
cuddle-and-hold doll.
I need to find her and
kiss her good night!"

"Come out, my sweet doll,
my under-the-sheet doll.
Come meet the new doll,
Nellie, my Nell."

"I can sleep tight now.
Everything's right now,

snuggled up close to my

very best doll."